THE PRIME OF
TAMWORTH PIG

Gene Kemp

Illustrated by Carolyn Dinan

faber and faber

LONDON · BOSTON

First published in 1972
by Faber and Faber Limited
3 Queen Square London WC1N 3AU
Published with 'Tamworth Pig Saves the Trees' in 1987
as *Tamworth Pig Stories*
This paperback edition first published in 1989

Printed in Great Britain by
Richard Clay Ltd, Bungay, Suffolk

British Library Cataloguing in Publication Data is available

ISBN 0-571-15345-3

For Eva
With love and thanks

The Prime of Tamworth Pig

Gene Kemp was born in Wigginton, a small Midland village outside Tamworth, whose famous pigs she celebrates in *The Prime of Tamworth Pig*, her first book for children.

After several books about this wonderful pig and his friends, she broke new ground with her school story, *The Turbulent Term of Tyke Tiler* which was awarded the Library Association's Carnegie Medal in 1978. In 1984 she was awarded an honorary Master of Arts degree in recognition of her achievement as a writer of children's books.

Gene Kemp now lives in Exeter. She is married with three children and has two grand-daughters.

by the same author

Stories about Cricklepit Combined School

THE TURBULENT TERM OF TYKE TILER
(Awarded the Library Association's Carnegie Medal)

GOWIE CORBY PLAYS CHICKEN

CHARLIE LEWIS PLAYS FOR TIME

JUNIPER

JASON BODGER AND THE PRIORY GHOST

NO PLACE LIKE

I CAN'T STAND LOSING

DOG DAYS AND CAT NAPS

MR MAGUS IS WAITING FOR YOU

THE CLOCK TOWER GHOST

THE WELL

TAMWORTH PIG AND THE LITTER

CHRISTMAS WITH TAMWORTH PIG

Edited by Gene Kemp

DUCKS AND DRAGONS
Poems for Children

Ah! Tamworth Pig is a very fine pig
  The best you'll ever see,
His ears stand up, his snout is long,
  His score is twenty-three.
He's wise and good and big and bold,
  And clever as can be,
A faithful friend to young and old
  The Pig of Pigs is he.

By courtesy of Mr. Rab

". . . Pigs of the Tamworth breed . . . are creatures of enchantment. . . ."

Anonymous pig-fancier

Chapter One

*

Thomas sat on top of a grassy hill on a warm, windy, April afternoon.

"Yoicks," he shouted into the breeze.

He felt wonderful, having just recovered from mumps, measles, chicken-pox, German measles, scarlatina and whooping cough. But, at last, he was better; there didn't appear to be much left to catch and the doctor had said he needn't go back to school till September.

"Just let him run wild," were his words.

"If he's at home running wild, then I shall go to school to keep out of his way," Daddy had replied.

Thomas bellowed to the fields and hedges all around:

> *"No more school, mouldy old school,*
> *No more school and sorrow,*
> *Lots and lots of holidays*
> *Before there comes tomorrow."*

He rolled over and over down the hill at the sheer bliss of his thought, followed closely by Hedgecock and Mr. Rab who were arguing as usual.

"You're not in the least like a real rabbit. Don't make me laugh."

"Yes, I am. I am. Say I am, please. Just a bit like one."

Hedgecock snorted loudly.

"I never saw a real rabbit with a red and white striped waistcoat, a green bow tie, and skinny, pink, furry legs. You're enough to make a cat laugh—to say nothing of a real rabbit."

"Well, what about you? What are you, then? A hedgecock with feathery prickles. You can't fly and you can't prickle."

"But I'll tell you what I can do. I can bash you, Stripey."

He proceeded to do so. Mr. Rab roared with pain. He was no match for Hedgecock.

"Stop that," Thomas commanded. "I'll do the bashing round here. Come on. What shall we do?"

"The stream," Hedgecock said. "We'll go to the stream."

"Yes, to the stream; let's go."

They ran over the grass, Mr. Rab trying to dodge the daisies; he was soft-hearted over flowers, over everything in fact, except Hedgecock, and he hated treading on daisies.

Suddenly they were there. Banks, two or three feet high, covered with mossy rocks just right for sitting on, bordered the clear water. The trio sniffed eagerly. It smelt good, as ever. Perhaps it was the bracken, or the wild thyme, or perhaps it was just the stream itself that gurgled over the brown stones on the sandy bed. The path ran into a curving bay and stepping-stones crossed to the other side. Farther down there was a

10

stretch of grassy turf covered with molehills and mole-holes. Thomas walked into the water, still with his shoes and socks on, and tried to catch minnows shooting this way and that. Then he sat down on a stone and contemplated his feet (over which the stream rippled making very interesting patterns) for some time.

"I know, let's make a dam," he said at last.

They chose a spot where the stream narrowed between high banks. Hedgecock worked steadily, counting the large stones (four-five-six-seven-eight-nine-ten-eleven) as he carried them to Thomas, who rammed them into position against the log they'd pushed across the stream. Mr. Rab was ordered to plaster mud and sand into the gaps. He whimpered to himself, for the water was cold and his paws hurt. Water still rushed through the spaces between the stones but its colour was turning to a reddish-brown, and gradually it slowed down and began to spread out on the flat, grassy ground above the dam.

Mr. Rab sat on a rock, tucking his wet paws under his waistcoat, and stuck his thin legs into the sun-warmed grass. The other two ignored him, as they continued to stuff pebbles, mud and grass into every crack. Mr. Rab began to recite in his special voice that he kept for poetry, which was a kind of high, wobbly moan.

> "*There's a stream on a grassy common*
> *Runs very swift and clear. . . .*"

"You can cut that lot out," Hedgecock shouted. "I hate your rotten poetry. If you've enough energy to say that old rubbish, then you'd better come and help."

But Mr. Rab wasn't listening. "Look! Look!" he shrieked.

The others turned round to see why he was dancing about and pointing a quivering paw. Upstream of the dam, the water was now several feet wide and all the moleholes had disappeared beneath it. There on the grass, shaking their fists, were dozens of angry moles.

"You horrible beasts," the Chief Mole shouted, leaping from one damp foot to the other. "You've wrecked our homes. You nearly drowned us all."

"We didn't mean . . ." Thomas began.

"Yes you did. You did it on purpose. I know you. We all know you. Terrible Thomas, that's who you are; you—you—you——"

The mole spluttered with rage and wetness.

Mr. Rab was dashing the tears from his eyes and Hedgecock was trying to hide in the bracken.

"I'm sorry," Thomas muttered. "We'll undam: I mean, we'll knock it down. Hedgecock, stop creeping away. Come and help."

With one accord, they and the moles all began to demolish the dam. It came down much faster than it went up, Hedgecock noted bitterly. Soon the stream was flowing as noisily and happily as before.

"It will be all right now," the Chief Mole said. "We shall dry out in the sun. I don't think you meant it after all."

"No, we didn't."

"Next time, build farther up there and then it won't affect us."

"But will there be a next time?" Mr. Rab moaned. "Look at us."

Silently they inspected one another: wet, scratched, plastered with mud. Thomas had torn his trousers and lost his shoes and socks.

"Come on, there's going to be trouble," he said.

At that moment two figures leapt from the bank and pushed Thomas flat into the stream. Even as his head was held down into the cold water, while their feet kicked him, Thomas knew who they were—Christopher Robin Baggs (most unsuitably named), a spotty boy with stick-out teeth, and his rough, tough friend, Lurcher Dench, both enemies of Thomas. He had fought many battles with them, but he had thought they were at school today, and so he had not been on the look-out. He squirmed and struggled and kicked under their combined weight. Then one of them stood on his legs. It hurt.

"Let's drown old Twopenny Tom," they were yelling. "Down with Measle Bug."

Somehow he got his face out of the water. Hedge-cock was snapping and biting but Mr. Rab had disappeared. The rage inside Thomas was bubbling like a boiling cauldron. Fancy letting himself be caught like this and without shoes. He couldn't have been more defenceless. The terrible thought shot through his head that perhaps they really did intend to drown him, as Lurcher once more ground his face down into the sand and water. There was a roaring in Thomas's ears and stars shot across the blankness that was enveloping him. The roaring crescendoed into a mighty sound that was somehow not in his head and as if by magic, the weight lifted off him, the kicks and blows and the pain ceased, and he stood up shakily to see the backs of his attackers running away as if pursued by demons. Mr. Rab's soft paws were stroking his sore legs as Thomas stumbled forward to his rescuer.

There on the bank stood a huge, golden pig, a giant of a pig, the colour of beech leaves in autumn, with upstanding, furry ears and a long snout.

"Tamworth!" Thomas gasped, spitting out water, sand and the odd tooth. "Oh! Tamworth, I am pleased to see you. How did you know?"

"Mr. Rab fetched me—ran like the wind, he did. I

14

wasn't far away. Funny the way those two objection-
able boys fled when they saw me. I can't think why.
I'm a most amiable animal and I don't believe in
violence."

"I ache all over," Thomas said, investigating his
bruises.

"Up on my back, all of you. Home we must go.
Your mother will undoubtedly have a few words to
say. Humph! Don't wet all my bristles."

"Giddy-up, Tamworth," Thomas said, holding
tight to the golden back.

Thomas's mother did, in fact, have a great many
things to say when he arrived home; she went on and
on for a considerable time. Later, he lay very carefully

in bed because of his many bruises, and buried his face in Num. To everyone else, Num was just a piece of shabby, grey blanket but to Thomas, Num was warmth and softness and comfort in times of sorrow. Wriggling gingerly into the welcoming folds, he said to Mr. Rab:

"Sing a bedtime song."

"Not that old muck," Hedgecock growled.

"Go and count your squares if you don't want to hear it."

Hedgecock retired muttering to the blanket of knitted squares at the foot of the bed. There were eight one way and ten the other, all in different

colours. Hedgecock loved to count them in tens, or twos, or ones.

Mr. Rab sang reedily. This was a special poem and he'd made up a tune to it, of which he was very proud.

> *"Mr. Rab has gone to sleep*
> *Tucked in his tiny bed*
> *He has curled up his furry paws*
> *And laid down his sleepy head."*

"Seventy-eight, seventy-nine, eighty," droned Hedgecock. Then there was a loud snore as he, like the others, fell asleep.

Chapter Two

————————————*————————————

Blossom, Thomas's sister, had a day's holiday from school and so got up very early, full of cheer. She laid the breakfast, took tea to Mummy and Daddy and then woke up Thomas to play a game of Monopoly. Thomas liked games but hated to lose and he hated paying out any money so from time to time he would rush from the room roaring and stamping with rage. Then, having simmered down, he would come back.

Blossom remained quite unperturbed by all this, merely continuing with her book till his return. She was a round, brown-eyed girl, rather like an otter, with an amiable disposition and a kind heart. Like Mr. Rab she loved poetry and hated sums. She couldn't understand, at all, Thomas's wish to win everything. In a good game winning didn't matter. She was as warm and comfortable as a bed at the end of a tiring day and sometimes silly, with a great and glorious silliness, just to show she wasn't too saintly after all.

The game came to an end with Thomas hurling the board across the room as he was obviously going to lose. Money, dice, tokens, houses, hotels flew through the air.

"I hate that stupid game," he shouted.

"Only because you're losing," Blossom said calmly, picking up the debris.

They then went down to breakfast, and afterwards set off for Baggs's orchard to see Tamworth Pig, for he always welcomed visitors and conversation. Tamworth belonged to Farmer Baggs, whom he liked, but was looked after by Mrs. Baggs—a mean woman— whom he hated. Christopher Robin Baggs we have already encountered. His warfare with Tamworth and Thomas had gone on for a long time, dating probably from the time when he'd tried to set fire to Tamworth's straw to see how quickly the pig could move. Actually it was Christopher who did the moving, pursued by an inflammatory Tamworth.

When Blossom and Thomas arrived, Tamworth was deep in conversation with Joe the Shire-horse.

"The price of pig food has gone up again, Joe. It's ridiculous. Mrs. Baggs hardly gives me a decent meal as it is, just a lot of old scraps, scarcely sufficient to maintain a budgerigar in good health. Now I suppose she'll give me even less. Hello, Blossom. Hello, Thomas. Have you heard? The price of pig food is up, and eggs and butter are to cost more. And this isn't necessary. The economic situation of this country is due entirely to inefficiency. Now, if I were Prime Minister, everything would soon be different."

"Why? What would you do then?" Joe asked slowly.

New ideas were always difficult for Joe.

"Well, I'd put the most important thing first."

"And what's that?"

"Why, food, of course," Tamworth said. "We can't live without food. We can't work without food. Food keeps us going and I also think it's one of the best things in life. The very best possibly."

"I believe you're right," Blossom agreed.

She felt in her anorak pocket for a toffee that she seemed to remember leaving there, for she dearly loved to eat.

"I've brought some apples for you."

Thomas emptied the contents of his brown paper bag on the floor.

"They're a bit wormy, but all right."

Tamworth gobbled them down and then continued speaking.

"Well, then, since food is the most important thing in life we should gear our whole existence to its production. Think, for example, of all the waste ground in this country. It should all be used to grow more food, potatoes, mushrooms, peas, lettuce, tomatoes, onions and lovely cabbage. Children should be taught to grow and make as much food as possible. Everyone could make more sweets, toffees and chocolates, and cakes, and biscuits, and buns and bread, and there would be lots and lots for everyone. We could even send tons of food abroad to feed the starving people."

"What about the 'orses?" Joe asked. "What about my 'ay?"

Joe had a one-track mind which seldom moved far from the thought of hay.

"Tons of hay go to waste every year on the grass verges by the sides of the roads. It should all be used. Extra food, better food could then be given to all the cows and hens, who would give more butter, cheese and eggs. More of everything for everybody except MEAT. Meat," Tamworth repeated firmly, "is bad for everyone."

Tamworth's feelings about meat were very strong.

"Yes, that should be our country's motto. MAKE

MORE FOOD. And if I ever become Prime Minister, it will be the first point on my programme."

"GROW MORE GRUB would sound better," Thomas suggested.

A voice was heard calling for Joe and he lumbered away, brooding on the prospect of unlimited hay.

"Tamworth," Blossom said slowly, "you're known as a very wise pig. Tell me, how can we make some money?"

"Why do you ask?"

"Well, you know, I think we must be very poor because every time I want something, Mummy says, 'Do you think I'm made of money?' and Daddy's always grumbling about bills and income tax. And then Gwendolyn Twitchie has twice as much pocket money as I do."

"And you have twice as much as me," Thomas grumbled. "It's not fair."

"I'm older than you."

"Yes, but you're much more stupid, so I ought to get as much as you."

"Stop arguing," Tamworth commanded. "I shall have to give this some thought. Have you got another apple?"

"No, you've eaten them all."

"Well, it's time for my morning nap now. Call again soon and I'll let you know if I've thought of anything. Oh, and can you draw lots of posters with 'Make More Food' on them, and I'll get them distributed. I feel I must start a campaign, in view of this rise in the price of pig food."

He turned round twice in his comfortable quarters, pushed his straw into a heap and flopped down.

"Scratch my back, please, Thomas. The stick's over there."

Thomas scratched the bristly, golden back and Tamworth closed his eyes in contentment. Soon a gentle, whiffling noise filled the air.

"He's asleep," Blossom whispered.

Tamworth opened one small, bright eye.

"I'm not. I'm thinking, Good-bye."

They wandered slowly home. The sun was shining. It was a beautiful day.

"Let's play in the tree-house with Hedgecock and Mr. Rab," Thomas said.

"All right."

And they raced back to the house singing "Green grow the rushes-oh!"

24

After that the day suddenly went wrong for Thomas, for who should be awaiting Blossom but Gwendolyn Twitchie. Instantly Blossom turned into a different creature.

"Let's be princesses," they squawked and ran giggling into the bedroom.

Thomas banged on the door and shouted, "Let me in, you stupid fools!" but they only tittered and piled things against the door so that he couldn't shift it at all. He fetched his hammer in order to batter it down, but Daddy appeared, roaring like a lion. He sent Thomas into the garden, where he wandered dismally into the tree-house with Mr. Rab and Hedgecock. They couldn't seem to start off a good game, but sat arguing feebly, making patterns in the dust with their shoes.

Suddenly Daddy came up to them.

"You seem miserable, Thomas. Oh, yes, of course, Blossom's got that awful child with her. Here, go and buy yourself something with this."

Thomas ran to the nearest shop, where he purchased a particularly sticky bar of toffee which he ate all over the house, putting his fingers everywhere. He didn't realize he was doing this; he was just thinking of all the horrible names he would like to call Gwendolyn, but Mummy found the traces.

"Look at the mess you've made and the hall's just been painted. Now go upstairs and wash your hands, and clean your teeth while you're about it. They're like yellow fangs."

The toothpaste was minty and frothy. Thomas used a lot of it, building up a fine lather. He stuck his head out of the window and surveyed the garden. Everything was growing beautifully and he could see the most marvellous red and yellow tulip.

"I wonder if I can spit in it?" he thought, leaning far out of the window and taking careful aim.

At that very moment, Daddy chose to walk along the path and the frothy cloud dropped on his head and started to trickle into his eyes. The roar this time was really awe-inspiring, like fifty lions. Thomas crouched down under the bathroom window. Too late he thought of seeking refuge elsewhere. Daddy, like an avenging Thor with his thunderbolt, loomed large and terrible in the doorway, wiping off large quantities of toothpaste.

"Bed," he remarked grimly, "is the only place for you today."

He scooped Thomas under one arm, carried him into his room and dumped him on the bed.

"Don't dare get up till I tell you."

He closed the door and stamped off.

Thomas lay in misery. All the beauty of the day had gone. Mr. Rab crept down beside him and tried to sing the bedtime song.

"Shut up, you idiot. It's morning."

Hedgecock was counting up to a thousand in tens, but Thomas didn't care. He buried his face in Num and tried to sleep.

He was allowed up for lunch and sat quietly while Gwendolyn and Blossom chattered gaily. Gwendolyn was the daughter of Blossom's teacher and was said to be very clever.

26

"I'm reading a very difficult book just now," she informed them all.

Blossom looked at her admiringly. Thomas pushed his plate away, for Gwendolyn put him off his food, and, besides, he was very full of toffee.

After lunch he put out his lines for Percy, the small engine, and watched him, but the busy, chuffing train could not hold his attention for long. He heard the girls laughing in the garden and he lay on his back and drummed with his heels. Mr. Rab tried to pat his head but he pushed the soft paw away. Then Mummy came in.

"I thought we'd have a picnic on the lawn as it's such a lovely day. Oh, do stop kicking, Thomas, and cheer up."

Thomas sat up.

"Can we have ice-cream and sausages on sticks and cheesy biscuits?"

"Yes, of course. Now will you cheer up?"

"Mummy, take me to the stream. Just me. Please."

She considered this for a moment.

"All right. Just for a little while. Come on, then."

And suddenly, the day was beautiful once more. Cares forgotten, Thomas rushed to the stream, took off his shoes and socks this time, and paddled in the water. Mummy read and dozed. Mr. Rab picked some flowers and Hedgecock floated twigs downstream.

> *"Winter's short,*
> *Summer's long,*
> *Let's all sing*
> *A Flowering song!"*

27

warbled Mr. Rab.

"Twenty-one, twenty-two, twenty-three," Hedge-cock grunted.

At last Mummy got up, rather slowly, for it was pleasant on the warm, soft grass.

"If we're going to have our picnic tea, I'd better go and get it ready," she said.

They walked home in the sunny afternoon and Mummy went into the kitchen. The voices of Gwendolyn and Blossom on the lawn sounded just a little peevish. They were quarrelling as to which one was to be the chief princess. A day spent in each other's company had been too much, and Blossom had begun to wish that she'd gone to the stream instead of listening to a long recital of Gwendolyn's cleverness and achievements.

Thomas squatted in a far corner of the lawn and began to make a worm collection. Glorious things, worms. Daddy had told him how useful they were in the garden. He and Hedgecock tried to straighten them out to see which one was the longest. It's not easy straightening wiggly, wriggly worms but very interesting if you happen to like them, which Mr. Rab didn't.

> *"A wriggling worm*
> *Just makes me squirm,"*

he shuddered.

Thomas and Hedgecock took no notice. The worms felt cool and smooth, and there were lots of them.

"Thirty-three, thirty-four, thirty-five," Hedgecock counted.

Gwendolyn could not resist; over she came to the counting figures.

"Ooeeowh," she squealed. "How horrid. How nasty. Oh, you are a dirty, beastly little boy, aren't you, Thomas?"

He didn't reply, having just found a good cluster under the apple tree, but Gwendolyn went on.

"I've heard a lot about you. Blossom says how awful you are."

Blossom's cheeks began to go red. She was squirming inside, just like Mr. Rab, only not because of the worms which she didn't mind at all. She'd realized that she much preferred Thomas to Gwendolyn, and remembered the tree-house and his anger and disappointment when he'd been shut out of the games. Gwendolyn was going on and on, as she always did when she got started on a topic.

"Fifty-four, fifty-five, fifty-six," Thomas counted. Mr. Rab sang under his breath:

> *"Gwendolyn's a silly twit,*
> *I don't like her one little bit."*

"I should hate to have you for a brother," Gwendolyn shrilled on.

Blossom thought her voice sounded like a dentist's drill, and she half hoped that Thomas would explode in one of his furies, but feared what would happen if he did.

"Why, you don't even say hedgehog, you say hedgecock. I've heard you. A hedgecock, I ask you!" Gwendolyn twittered gaily.

Thomas looked up at her curls bobbing up and down, pale blonde curls like corkscrews. "Just like worms," he thought, and, seizing his collection, he threw them with careful aim all over her face and hair.

Mother had always had a gift for appearing at the wrong moment. Bearing a tray of food she was just in time to see and hear Gwendolyn screaming hysterically, brushing off hordes of worms.

"I'm never coming here again," she shrieked as she rushed away.

"Blossom, go after her and apologize to her. I know he won't," Mother said as she put down the tray.

"Oh Thomas, how could you? Why on earth did you?"

He stood sullen and silent, but Blossom, her face crimson, cried:

"It was her fault. He wasn't doing anything and she went on and on, saying nasty things, and laughing at Thomas because of Hedgecock."

She stopped and burst into tears.

"Well, Thomas?"

"I'm sorry—a bit."

"You don't throw worms at people, however badly they behave. Blossom, there's a box of chocolates at the top of the cupboard. Run after her and say Thomas is sorry and give her the box. Then we'll have our tea out here. It's a pity to waste it. But, Thomas, go and wash your hands. I don't share your fondness for worms."

> *"Oh lovely, shiny, frabjous day*
> *Gwendolyn has gone away,"*

carolled Mr. Rab.

"There were fifty-nine worms altogether," Hedgecock announced. "Shall I let them go?"

"Yes," they all shouted together.

Chapter Three

———————————— * ————————————

Blossom and Thomas had awoken early and begun on the posters requested by Tamworth Pig. Hedgecock assisted, but Mr. Rab still lay in bed, nose a-twitch, dreaming of living in a burrow with real rabbits, his favourite dream. Blossom's posters were beautiful, neatly lettered, and decorated with drawings of grapes and apples, and the hives of honey-bees. Thomas's were covered with finger marks and large wobbly letters that wandered up and down the paper. Blossom's read "Make more Food", and Thomas's "Grow more Grub". Hedgecock was doing some of his own on rather tatty torn-off scraps. "Vote for T. Pig of Baggs's Farm" he wrote. He also counted them. Blossom had done twelve, very neatly, Thomas nineteen, rather messily, and Hedgecock seven.

"I wish I hadn't got to go to school," Blossom moaned. "I'd like to deliver these to Tamworth now, not wait till four o'clock."

"That's simple," Hedgecock replied. "Don't go."

"Oh, but I must."

"Why?"

"To learn."

Hedgecock snorted. "You can read and write and

draw, now. You'll never learn to do sums any more than Mr. Rab will. And Tamworth can tell you more than anybody. He knows everything. School is Mrs. Twitchie. Ugh!"

Mr. Rab woke up in the middle of the speech, rubbing his eyes.

"What was all that about?"

"Hedgecock says it's no good going to school."

"Oh, but he's so wrong, so very wrong, as usual," Mr. Rab quavered, ignoring Hedgecock's fierce glare. "First of all, you have to learn to be good, you see. That's the most important lesson. And you can't really learn it at home, because you have to learn to mix with other people, and like them. Even the horrid ones. You see, they have just as much right to be them as you have to be you. Hedgecock and Thomas just think that what they think is right, is right, if you see what I mean. Don't hit me."

Hedgecock did hit him, and Mr. Rab cried, but he spoke on bravely.

"I know if I'd ever been to school, I wouldn't be so shy with real rabbits. I'd be able to be friends with them."

Thomas put down the posters.

"When you two have finished, she'll have to go 'cos she'll get walloped if she doesn't. Now shut up. You can come with me to take them to Tamworth."

"Don't forget to ask him about making money, he must have some ideas by now," Blossom said as they went down to eat their breakfast.

Tamworth was pleased to see them. He was running

happily around his half-acre of land, most of which was trampled down and eaten clean of grass, flowers, shoots, thistles, nettles—the lot. Pigs are wonderful at clearing ground. They often have to have rings in their snouts to stop them destroying too much, but Tamworth wasn't ringed. Mr. Baggs had considered it, but on seeing the look in Tamworth's eyes had refrained from doing so.

Thomas had brought two carrier bags with him, one containing the posters, the other some apples and potato peelings. Tamworth was pleased with the apples, but the peelings he regarded with disdain. He ate them all the same.

"Sorry to be ungracious, dear Thomas. It's just that Mrs. Baggs, that extremely mean woman, gives them to me all the time. Hardly ever do I get any proper pig food. Swill, I believe they call it. A nasty word. I do wish that people would realize that we pigs are essentially clean, fastidious animals. We suffer because of the lazy, inefficient methods of humans. Now if I were Prime Minister, it would all be changed. You see. . . ."

Thomas brought out the posters from his bag in order to stop Tamworth, who seemed likely to go on for ever.

"It's a day for people making long speeches."

Thomas himself believed in action, not words.

Tamworth examined the posters.

"Mm. Not bad. Not bad at all. Blossom's are very nice. Refined. They give tone to the whole proceeding. Those are yours, Thomas, I suppose. Well, we must be grateful for small mercies. Still, they'll do.

Hedgecock, I presume these are yours. Quite hideous, but the idea's good. I'd like them copied by Blossom, with my name in full and with a portrait of me on them—in profile."

"What's profile?" Thomas asked.

"Sideways on," Hedgecock hissed back. "Showing his snout and tail."

"Quite right, though somewhat inelegantly expressed. Perhaps our great poet Mr. Rab may pen a few rhymes in my honour and we can write them on a poster."

Mr. Rab simpered with delight and started rhyming immediately.

> *Vote for Pig*
> *He's really big.*
> *Tamworth—er—hamworth."*

Hedgecock kicked him.

"What 'ave we got to vote for you for, anyway?" Joe said, ambling from nowhere into the morning. "'Ave we got an animals' Parliament or summat? And will it get me more oats and 'ay?"

Tamworth sat silent as though thunderstruck. At last he spoke.

"Of course, of course. Out of the mouths of hedgecocks and horses cometh wisdom. You've hit it."

He snorted three times.

"That's it. I'll be President of the Animals' Parliament. I think someone thought of something similar. George, his name was. But I shall do better—much better."

He charged three times round his ground and sat down again, breathless.

"On with the posters, Thomas. Joe, get together all the animals you can muster and tell all the pigeons, owls, sparrows and starlings—yes, especially the starlings—they're a chatty crowd—that there's a meeting in the orchard, tonight, at midnight. Spread the word."

"By the way," Thomas said, before Tamworth got too carried away, "Blossom told me to ask about the money."

"What money?"

Tamworth was occupied with a vision of himself as the chief animal of the British Isles.

"We want to get some money because Mummy and Daddy are poor."

Thomas sounded bored but it was only because he'd already explained this and he hated wasting words.

"Oh, that. Well, a little money can be earned easily, like this. Gather some wild flowers, tie a ribbon round them, put them in water—jam jars will do—and sit by the roadside and sell them. Trippers will buy them, telling their friends they picked them in the wild woods and then do quite nasty flower arrangements at home with two twigs and a piece of bark."

"I don't fancy that," Thomas said.

"Blossom and I will do it," Mr. Rab volunteered.

"Well, then, Thomas. You know Ethelberta Ever-Ready, the hen that lays so many? She has a secret nest by the old barn that isn't used any more and Mrs. Baggs, that mean woman of whom you've doubtless heard me speak, hasn't found it yet. Ethelberta keeps on laying and laying and there are dozens of eggs there. Show them by the roadside with a special poster saying 'Extra fresh eggs here in the countryside', and motorists will buy them for far more than they would pay in the shops."

"What about half as much again?" Hedgecock the mathematician asked.

"That would be excellent," Tamworth said.

"We'll do that. Good-bye. Thanks, Tamworth."

"Are you coming to the meeting?"

"No, it's too late, but I'll come and hear about it later."

"More oats and 'ay is what I'll say," Joe promised.

Tamworth was walking up and down composing speeches as they left.

They meandered through the fields for some time, then followed the ditches home, swatting nettles and flies with their sticks. Thomas stopped to cut off a stem of hedge-parsley to make a blowpipe to blow the hawthorn buds through. And out of the corner of his eye he saw a flash of red jersey on the other side of the hedge.

"Look out," he whispered to Hedgecock. "Robin Redbreast is about."

Quietly they ran along to climb the stile that led into the next field, and crouching behind the hedge were Christopher Robin and Lurcher Dench, preparing to jump him. Thomas's face was crimson, his eyes shining with excitement. He stepped to one side to avoid Christopher's mis-timed rush, putting out his foot very neatly to trip him head first into the nettle-

filled, watery ditch, There was a despairing wail from
Christopher as his face encountered mud, weed, snails,
nettles and the bramble.

Thomas turned to deal with Lurcher. Putting his
head down, he rushed at him and butted him in the
solar plexus. Lurcher fell back, winded, but not for
long. Recovering his breath, he rushed forward, arms
flailing like a windmill. Thomas knelt down and
Lurcher fell over him. Up he jumped, aiming kicks at
Thomas's shins and pulling his sweater so hard that the
seams parted down one side.

Hedgecock yelled: "Come on, Thomas. Bash him."

Lurcher kicked him out of the way. Then Thomas
went berserk. He charged at Lurcher, hitting left to the
head, right to the body and left to the nose, which was
bleeding as Lurcher stumbled away. He didn't cry.
But by now, Christopher Robin had emerged even
spottier from the nettles, shouting unprintable words

about what he was going to do to Thomas, who hit him firmly in one eye. Mrs. Baggs's boy departed howling.

"Come on," Thomas said. "Stop shivering, Mr. Rab. I'm all right."

"Yes, we won," Hedgecock said.

"Of course we did, we always shall, but I wonder what Mummy will say. She'll never believe I didn't start it."

She didn't.

He said to Tamworth Pig later that day as he sat curled up beside him with Num covering them both:

"Grown-ups are unfair, Tamworth."

"Something that you have to learn, Thomas, is the terrible injustice of life. Even you and I, deserving and worthy as we are, cannot win all the time."

Chapter Four

Whitsuntide holidays had come round and Blossom was to have a week at home. Money-making plans could be put into operation, but first Tamworth must be visited to see if he needed any further assistance in his campaign for "Grow more Grub but Eat less Meat".

Blossom had finished twenty "Vote for Tamworth Pig—He's really Big" posters. He looked most handsome in profile with his long snout and curling tail. They took these along with several offerings for Tamworth's enormous appetite. Hedgecock also hopefully took a chessboard. He was growing a little tired of posters and campaigns and wished he had never started the idea. Previously he had enjoyed a game of chess with Tamworth, but now the pig always seemed too busy.

Tamworth was trotting up and down under the damson tree.

"We've held our meeting," he said. "We've sent out the posters and animals are showing great interest. We've got in touch with farms over all the county. If I can get enough support to be elected President of the Animals' Parliament I shall approach the Minister of Agriculture and put our case before him."

VOTE FOR
TAMWORTH PIG

He's really BIG

"But how will you get to see him?" Blossom asked, practical as ever. "A pig can't walk into the Houses of Parliament."

Mr. Rab choked back a giggle as Tamworth frowned on him.

"No, I don't especially wish to go to London. I don't think I should care for the traffic. But we shall ask the Minister to come here. He's always willing to visit farms."

"Won't you play chess, instead?" Hedgecock asked. "The black knight is going quite green from not being used."

"I may play games again in the future, but, at present, I must dedicate myself to the Cause."

"You're really keen, aren't you, Tamworth?"

"There's not much point in doing anything unless you put your heart and soul into it. By the way, Jasper, that particularly black-hearted stallion, is putting his heart and soul into opposing me, aided and abetted by the miserable cur, Rover, the dog. We shall have to do something about them."

He distributed his great weight down in the most comfortable position.

"Good-bye. Time for my morning snooze."

He drifted off to sleep, a red-gold heap under the damson tree.

"Let's visit Ethelberta's nest and see if we can get some eggs to sell," Thomas said.

"You do that while I get my flower stall ready," Blossom said. "We'd better not choose a place too near home or Mummy will find out."

The next day was perfect, and, of the cars that streamed along the road, many stopped to buy "Pretty

Flowers", and "Fresher than Fresh Eggs from the Country". By evening they'd taken two pounds, according to Hedgecock, who kept the account.

They returned home flushed with pride, and hid the money in a tin at the bottom of Thomas's wardrobe.

"They're up to something," Mummy said, late that night.

Daddy put down his paper.

"What makes you think so?"

"They're so quiet. Something's up."

"If they are we'll soon find out. Thomas will do something he shouldn't and give the show away."

The weather remained sunny and the children had another good day. Wild flowers were blooming everywhere, and Ethelberta was still laying eggs at a great rate, so they had plenty of produce to sell. In all, the takings totalled four pounds and they sat in Thomas's room and discussed what they were going to do with the money. Blossom wrote down the final decision, which went like this.

> One pound to Tamworth Pig for the Fund.
> One pound to starving children.

"Better send that to Oxfam," Blossom had said.

> One pound to Mummy and Daddy as a present.
> One pound to spend on . . .

"Sweets, chocolates, crisps, ice-cream, lemonade," they all cried together.

Heavy footsteps sounded on the stairs.

"It's Daddy," Blossom whispered. "Hide the tin."

A hasty scuffle followed and Blossom shoved the tin under the pillow as the door opened to reveal both Mummy and Daddy.

"Mrs. Baggs has just called. She says you've been taking their eggs to sell at the roadside. Gwendolyn Twitchie told her."

"She would," Thomas muttered.

"Is this true?" Daddy asked in a stern voice.

"They're Ethelberta's eggs, not Mrs. Baggs's."

"Ethelberta belongs to Mrs. Baggs and so do her eggs. Anyway, Mrs. Baggs was obviously telling the truth. Stop crying, Blossom, and tell me how much money you got for them."

They brought out the tin from under the pillow and made a hasty calculation, helped by Hedgecock. Blossom's tears fell all over the money, damping a very beautiful new pound note.

"We got two pounds for the eggs and two pounds for the wild flowers."

"Oh, so you've been selling wild flowers too?"

"Yes," Blossom howled. "We didn't think it was wrong. We only wanted to make some money 'cos we're so poor. We were going to give some to you."

Daddy and Mummy looked at one another.

"We're not so poor that you have to take other people's eggs and sell them. Give the money to me," Daddy said.

"You can keep the flower money," Mummy said. "But the rest must go to Mrs. Baggs."

"That horrible mean woman," Thomas muttered. "I bet she won't give any of it to Tamworth."

45

"What's that, Thomas?"

"Nothing."

"Don't mumble, boy. And Blossom, don't sell too many flowers. Much of the countryside is being ruined by people picking too many flowers. At this rate there'll be none left."

Mummy and Daddy went downstairs with the tin. The little band sat in a miserable heap on the bed.

"Never mind, we've still got two pounds left," Mr. Rab said.

"Yes, but it doesn't feel the same," Blossom wailed. "It doesn't feel nice any more."

"Two pound notes must feel nice, only four pounds felt better," Hedgecock growled. "More is always better than less."

"More school isn't better than less school," Thomas said.

"I think Mr. Rab's right," Blossom said. "We've still got a pound for Tamworth and a pound for ourselves."

Chapter Five

———————————*———————————

Uncle Jeff and Aunt Cynthia came for a holiday. Blossom loved them, but Thomas detested them. Mummy never seemed very cheery either during their visit, perhaps because she was always in the kitchen, cooking. Uncle Jeff liked lots of food. He was Daddy's brother and they laughed a lot together.

There were lots of people detested by Thomas, but on his special list of hates, Mrs. Baggs came first, Gwendolyn Twitchie second, Christopher Robin Baggs third and Aunt Cynthia fourth.

She was unusually tall and thin with elongated bones sticking out in all directions, and fuzzy, pink hair like candy floss. She was very proud of her hair and was always washing it, after which she would walk round in green plastic rollers looking like a creature from outer space. Her finger-nails were long, polished and pointed like daggers and almost as dangerous. She piled her dressing-table with jars and perfumes and talcum powder and bottles and brushes. When Thomas was very young, about four, he had crept into her room and covered himself with cream and powder and then drawn faces all over the mirror with lipstick and mascara. He thought it looked very pretty, but no one agreed with this idea. Aunt Cynthia had never liked him after that, not that she'd ever been very fond of him, anyway.

"Nasty, rude, spoilt little boy," she squeaked to Uncle Jeff.

Every year Thomas hoped she wouldn't come, but she always did, and he would watch her waggling walk and try not to listen to her high-pitched, niminy-piminy voice and think how nasty she was, especially when Blossom, who always copied other people's mannerisms, started to waggle and squeak too.

"It's really horrible," he said to Hedgecock.

Everyone else had gone shopping and they were playing with the green rollers, which they'd found in a polythene bag on the mantelpiece. They'd made them into forts, pretended they were soldiers, or, by putting them on their spiky sides, turned them into barbed-wire barricades. They arranged them in fives and eights, counting them happily. There were thirty-seven.

"A peculiar number," Hedgecock said. "There's always something over when you put it into twos or threes or fives or anything. There's others like it: thirteen or nineteen fr'instance. They ought to have a special name. Tamworth will know what it is."

They arranged them in a pattern on the flat top of the guard that was always bolted round the fire. Aunt Cynthia felt the cold, so there were constant hot fires despite the warm weather.

They went out into the garden. Time passed and then there came an appalling scream from the house.

48

Thomas sat back on his heels, listening with interest. Something was obviously going on.

Aunt Cynthia shot out of the door wailing like a cat with its tail trapped, and she bore down on Thomas.

"I'm going to slaughter you. I'm going to give you the hiding of a lifetime, you dreadful boy!"

Thomas did not stop to reason why. He leapt to his feet and fled as fast as he could go with Aunt Cynthia hot on his heels. But his legs were much shorter than her long ones, and in desperation he headed for Tamworth Pig, who was sitting in his favourite place under the damson tree.

"I shall catch you," Aunt Cynthia cried. "Don't think you can get away."

"Save me," Thomas panted as he scrambled on to the golden back.

Always ready to answer a cry for help, Tamworth heaved himself on to his trotters and Thomas held on for dear life. He pawed the ground, then charged full tilt with all his weight behind him at the rapidly approaching aunt. Her screams of rage changed into a different key as the Pig of Pigs hurtled towards her with Thomas clutching the furry ears. She spun around and, if anything, ran even faster back to home and safety.

"Horrible children and mad animals," she cried down on to Mummy's shoulder, which wasn't easy as she was much taller than Mummy, who finally got her off to bed with an aspirin.

Having settled the sorrowing aunt, she went to fetch

Thomas, who was now hiding between Tamworth and the damson tree, pretending not to be there.

"Tamworth," she remarked politely, handing him a pear, as he was an old friend of hers, "justice has to be done. Thomas must come home."

"Yes, I know, yet I am strangely reluctant to part with my young friend. Come out, Thomas."

Thomas lifted an unhappy face from behind the broad and sheltering back.

"I don't know what I'm supposed to have done."

"Just come in and I'll show you."

Thomas crept out slowly, slipped his hand into Mummy's and they went off together.

"Think of the Cause," Tamworth called after them. "Be brave, Thomas."

Thomas felt anything but brave. Mummy led him

to the fireguard, where lots of green blobs had spread, while others hung in dangling ringlets.

"Oh, the curlers melted."

"Yes," Daddy said, appearing from nowhere as he so often did. "When I've spanked you, you can go and apologize to Aunt Cynthia. Then, tomorrow, you can buy her some more with your pocket money."

Funnily enough, it wasn't a severe spanking, not one of Daddy's mightier efforts. He even seemed to be laughing a little. Perhaps he didn't like curlers either. Saying sorry was hard as it always is, especially to Aunt Cynthia. But it must have worked for she decided to stay a bit longer after all. She'd been packing her case when Mummy pushed him into the bedroom to make his speech.

"Just think," he said in bed that night. "If I'd refused to say sorry, she might have gone by now."

"Let's forget her," Hedgecock replied. "I was talking to Tamworth after you'd gone and he said those peculiar numbers like thirty-seven are called Prime numbers. Like Prime Pork, I said. Then he went all sulky and wouldn't talk to me."

"He hates you to mention pork or bacon or sausages," Mr. Rab said. "It makes him very sad. You are stupid, Hedgecock."

Hedgecock bashed Mr. Rab several times for that remark, but finally they all settled down to sleep.

Chapter Six

———————————— * ————————————

Uncle Jeff was quite a different shape from his wife, being tubby and bald, with a huge ginger moustache. He laughed a lot. He tickled Blossom under the chin and told her she was a smasher.

"That's right," Hedgecock muttered. "She's always breaking things."

Uncle Jeff sang as he helped with the washing up, and he sang as he came back from the "Duck and Dragon" with Daddy late at night. Daddy also sang, reported Mr. Rab, who never slept very soundly, unlike Hedgecock, who snored the dark away.

Blossom loved Uncle Jeff. She sat on his knee, wriggling and giggling as he asked:

"What key won't open a door?"

Blossom didn't know.

"A donkey, of course," he roared and they both fell on the floor with laughter. Cherry Blossom he called her.

He was very jolly with Thomas for three or four days, laughed and sang and told jokes, while his nephew remained unsmiling and expressionless, just staring at him. Actually he didn't think much of the jokes or the singing, but the ginger moustache he found fascinating.

"There's something peculiar about that boy of yours," Uncle Jeff said to Mummy, who was ironing. "I can't get on with him at all. He just sits and stares. Are you sure there's nothing wrong with him?"

"He isn't good with people," Mummy said, ironing fiercely and scorching something. "Oh bother." She sounded cross.

"I'm not people. After all, we come here every year and he never even says hello to me."

"Hello," Thomas said.

"Well, at least he understands what I say. I was beginning to wonder if he was quite right in the head."

Mummy banged down the iron.

"Thomas is quite clever and he understands everything you say."

"I wonder if they'll have a row," Mr. Rab whispered to Hedgecock.

They were sitting under the table waiting for Thomas to start a game but he was too busy gazing at the ginger moustache.

"I hope so."

Hedgecock loved rows, but, at that moment, Blossom burst in, her brown eyes shining, and flung herself at Uncle Jeff.

"Tell me a story," she cried.

"Did I tell you about the time I had to come down by parachute over enemy territory?"

"Hundreds of times," Daddy said, coming in for the paper and retreating with it hastily.

"No, he hasn't. Please tell me, Uncle Jeff. I want to hear."

"Well, I was in the Army, and one day a small group of us had to be transported to another unit by aeroplane. The weather was bad and we went off course, and, suddenly, this fighter appeared out of nowhere—guns firing—rat-tat-tat-tat. . . ."

Thomas came even nearer to watch the moustache.

"Were you frightened?" breathed Blossom.

"Scared stiff. They hit us and we were told to jump. . . ."

"From up in the air?"

"Yes. I was terrified the parachute wouldn't open."

"But it did," Thomas spoke up. "Or you'd have been all smashed up dead. Splattered all over the ground."

"Don't go on," Uncle Jeff said, looking pained.

"Where did you land?"

"In enemy territory. But a farmer hid me on his farm, smuggled me to the coast and I got a boat for England."

"Oh, you were brave."

Blossom's eyes were starry.

"Parachutes are nice things, like big balloons or umbrellas. Like big balloons or umbrellas," Thomas went on muttering to himself.

Next day he found a ladder and put it up to an outhouse roof. He was quiet and careful, as he didn't wish to be caught. Mr. Rab didn't like this new game at all for he was afraid of heights. After climbing up and down once or twice, Thomas fetched Blossom. She went up cheerfully, and they sat on the roof. Then Thomas crawled up to the chimney and produced two umbrellas from behind it, one a beautiful red and yellow one shaped like a pagoda, the other old and shabby.

Blossom looked horrified.

"What are you doing with those? That's Mummy's new one."

"Shan't hurt them. They're going to be our parachutes. We open them and jump off the roof. You can have the pretty one."

"Oh no, not me."

"It's quite safe. Look, Num's lying on the periwinkle bed to catch us."

Blossom looked down on the grey form of Num spread out apparently hundreds of feet below.

"No, I won't. I won't!"

She stood up, nearly fell off, and sat down again, hastily.

Thomas pushed his face close to hers, his eyes a hard blue stare.

"You took money from Mummy's purse. If you don't jump, I shall tell her."

"I gave some to you. Then I was sorry. I put it all back later and I never did it again."

Blossom cried in anguish, her face red, rocking noisily to and fro in her grief. Mr. Rab shut his eyes. He couldn't bear to look.

"She'll still be angry and sad, so jump."

"Jump," echoed Hedgecock.

"Don't," wept Mr. Rab.

"We'll hold umbrellas in one hand and each other's hands with the other," Thomas said.

Sad and tearstained, Blossom opened the glorious new umbrella. Thomas opened Daddy's greenish-black one. They stood up together and Blossom closed her eyes tight.

"I'm frightened," Mr. Rab wailed.

"Don't be silly. It's only a little jump," Hedgecock growled.

At that moment Mummy came round the corner just in time to see two figures leaping off the roof, one howling miserably. She saw her best umbrella blow inside out, and Blossom miss the soft comfort of Num and the periwinkle bed to fall heavily, her head striking a stone. She lay still, her face as white as it had been red earlier.

"Oh, oh," Mr. Rab shrieked.

"Trouble, trouble, trouble," Hedgecock groaned.

Blossom was not badly hurt, though she had to stay in bed for a few days. This time, Thomas wasn't spanked, but Mummy and Daddy talked long and seriously to him, and found out just why she had jumped when she was so afraid. Thomas promised to be a better boy. He really meant it, this time. In bed, at last, he held Num tightly and said:

"You were supposed to catch her too, Num."

"It's only your Num. It can't look after everyone," Mr. Rab said.

"Let's buy Blossom some sweets," Hedgecock suggested, which was a great concession for him as he was a mean animal.

Mr. Rab cheered up immediately.

"I'll write her a poem."

"Oh, no, there's no need to go that far," Hedgecock said, but Mr. Rab was away.

57

"Blossom high up on the roof,
  Terrified was she,
  Closed her eyes and then she fell
  Like a falling blossom from a tree."

"Oh, lumme, that's worse than usual," Hedgecock said and retired to the foot of the bed to count squares.

"I admit it's not very good, but it was on the spur of the moment."

Mr. Rab was always hurt by unkind remarks about his poems.

"Sing a bedtime song," Thomas whispered.

Mr. Rab sang, but for once its magic did not work and Thomas lay awake for a long time thinking of the difficulties of being a better boy until he too fell asleep to the gentle sound of Mr. Rab's snuffles and the monotonous whirring of Hedgecock's snores.

Chapter Seven

---

*

Thomas spent a miserable time while Blossom was in bed. He watched trays being carried up to her room, he saw the doctor running brightly up and down the stairs and Aunt Cynthia creeping about on the very tipmost of tiptoes, with finger ever at her lips motioning silence to everyone, especially him. Worst of all, Mummy had a worried, far-away look on her face which made it very difficult to go near her. She was always cooking, not making cakes or pies or rolling glorious strips of pastry, but simmering thin soups and beating up egg yolks. Whenever he dared to enter the kitchen he was immediately sent out to play. He wanted to go in and see Blossom and no one would let him, and he began to get the idea that she would die and it would all be his fault. Aunt Cynthia made it much worse.

"It's funny how such a little boy can cause such a lot of trouble," she shrilled. "Here you are, the smallest, the least of all of us, the last and youngest in the family and you cause more work and worry than the rest put together. I know what I'd do with you if I were your mother—I'd treat you like the nasty little baby you are, smack you hard, and send you to bed for a week, like poor, dear, sweet Blossom. The trouble with you is that you think you're important, whereas you come last in everything, or should do."

"Oh, do shut up, Cynthia," Uncle Jeff said, putting down his book. "Leave the boy alone."

He quite m. ¹ Thomas these days after the umbrella incident.

The boy in question wandered drearily away to find Tamworth Pig, who was fast asleep under his favourite tree. He put his head on the gently heaving fat form and felt comforted.

He and Hedgecock dozed off, but Mr. Rab stayed awake, nose and paws a-twitch. Minutes ticked slowly past, afternoon fashion. At last there was a convulsive heave as if someone were stirring a giant Christmas pudding. Tamworth was waking up. He rolled from side to side, then stood up abruptly, shaking his ears. Thomas and Hedgecock rolled over like a couple of ping-pong balls off a table, rubbed their eyes and were awake.

When they had finished yawning Tamworth said:

"I must tell you that we're having a special meeting tonight to vote Jasper or me as President. Will you come, this time? We need help to count the votes."

"Yes, I'll come," Hedgecock said. "I like counting."

"Well, Barry McKenzie Goat has offered to wait outside your house and bring you to the meeting."

"I'll come," Thomas said. "But Blossom can't. Oh, Tamworth, she isn't going to die, is she?"

"Of course not. What a silly idea. She'll live to be a hundred. Now, off you go, I've got to make up my speeches. Oh, Thomas, give my regards to Aunt Cynthia. She looked so funny when last I saw her."

He guffawed, and Thomas too began to smile, until he was bellowing with laughter as well. Soon they were all helpless with mirth under the damson tree.

When they arrived home, Mummy said:

"Blossom's asking to see you. You can go up and play after tea."

Sunlight exploded inside Thomas. He looked around, loving everyone.

"Hello, Uncle Jeff. Hallo, Aunt Cynthia. I'm glad you came to stay."

Uncle Jeff snorted into his teacup, blowing tea everywhere, and even Aunt Cynthia smiled.

Blossom had a marvellously huge bandage round her head. Mr. Rab was jealous so she made one for him as well. They sat on her bed while she read to

them from *The Wind in the Willows*. Then they acted it. Hedgecock was Badger, Blossom was Ratty, Mr. Rab was Mole and Thomas was Toad, of course.

After a while, Blossom felt tired, so Mummy took Thomas to bed, where he lay determined to stay awake for the meeting.

Chapter Eight

———————— * ————————

Thomas awoke with a start, for he had fallen asleep after all. He drew back the curtains and found it was already dark outside. He pulled a thick sweater and jeans over his pyjamas, and then put on his plimsolls so that he could move quietly. He draped Num around his neck, woke up the twitching Mr. Rab and the snoring Hedgecock, and they cautiously made their way downstairs, past Mummy's and Daddy's room where a light still showed under the door, and through the kitchen, silent but for the ticking of the clock. They pulled back the bolt, which made a grinding noise, and then out into the garden. It was so quiet that Thomas almost turned back but then he saw Barry McKenzie Goat's head peering over the wall, so he climbed over and put his hand on the hairy side.

"Come on, they're nearly ready to begin."

They hurried through the wet grass and into the orchard. There, by the light of flickering lanterns, sat cows, horses, sheep, pigs, goats, hens, turkeys, cats, ducks and dogs. There were even some rats and mice scurrying about and owls hooted in the trees.

Tamworth was seated under the damson tree, a magnificent sight in the lantern glow. On one side was

Joe the Shire Horse and Barry McKenzie Goat led Thomas to the other. The animals formed a great circle with Tamworth and Jasper, the stallion, at opposite ends of the diameter. Joe was Chairman, but was not very conspicuous. As Barry and Thomas took their places, Jasper was speaking in a rolling neigh.

"This idea of Tamworth's is absolutely worthless, useless and impractical. We shall never persuade our farming friends to sell less meat. Farmers make their money from selling animals for meat. We must just put up with this."

"Hear, hear," Rover barked.

He was a sheepdog and an especial favourite of Mrs. Baggs.

Tamworth rose to his trotters.

"Brother animals, brothers all," he cried. "We must remember that my black and spirited opponent here has hardly the same outlook as the rest of us, or most of us. If there is a chance that Brother Jasper may end up inside a dog-meat tin, that day is long distant, and as for our barking friend here, no one would ever contemplate eating him, a fact which I do not find at all surprising. But the rest of us tastier brothers are liable to be cut down in our prime, oh horrible word, at any time. However, this is only one point from my campaign. The main thing is that we must get the country to grow more food. If you support me in this and elect me as your President, I shall send an invitation to our Minister at the Houses of Parliament so that he may visit us and learn about our ideas."

"Hear, hear," Thomas shouted, quite carried away. "Grow more grub!"

Jasper turned to Rover.

"I do not think this young human should be present at a meeting of animals."

He glared with wild, rolling eyes at Thomas, who wrapped Num around himself and said:

"I am always on Tamworth's side——"

"On his back," Hedgecock hissed.

"—even if it does mean no roast ever."

It was easy for him. He hated roast. Poor Blossom would miss her Sunday dinner sadly if Tamworth had his way.

Jasper continued.

"Mr. Chairman, I wish to ask why this human is present tonight. I wish to object."

"Brother Thomas and Brother 'edgecock are 'ere to count votes. They don't 'ave any say theirselves. Objection over-ruled."

Tamworth had taught Joe "objection over-ruled" earlier in the day.

Barry McKenzie Goat stood up.

"I should like to propose Brother Tamworth as President of the Animals' Union, whose aim is to encourage more food growing in England for the good and happiness of all, including us animals."

He sat down again, and Joe spoke.

"Does anyone second this?"

Fanny Cow and Ethelberta Ever-Ready stepped forward.

"Proposal carried," Thomas said cheerfully.

Then Rover spoke.

"I propose Brother Jasper, the Black Stallion, as President of Follow the Farmers League, whose aim is to keep things exactly as they are."

Joe asked for a seconder and Rufus Pony and Pussy Cat stepped forward.

"Proposal carried. Will you please put up paw, 'oof, wing or claw to cast your vote? Brothers 'edgecock and Thomas, will you count for us?"

They would never have managed the counting without Hedgecock. With beady eyes a-glitter at such a task, he counted and counted, aided by Thomas.

"It's ninety-six votes to ninety-six votes for each candidate," he panted at last.

"A draw," the cows mooed. "What happens now?"

Tamworth spoke to Joe, who then stood up.

"Has Chairman, I 'ave the casting vote."

Everybody waited.

"I cast me Chairman's vote for Tamworth Pig!"

There was suddenly such a chorus of cheers, boos, neighs, moos, clucks, gobbles, squeals, roars, and howls that the lights all went on at Baggs's Farm.

"Quiet," Tamworth said, and they obeyed.

"Thank you for your confidence in me. I am deeply honoured. Now we must go home silently, lest there is trouble."

The animals melted quietly away into the shadows. Lanterns went out. Thomas felt very tired and he just wanted to curl up in Num and sleep under the damson tree, but Tamworth pushed him with his snout.

"Come on. Get on my back and I'll take you home."

He lowered himself and somehow Thomas scrambled on, and they went home. All the lights in the house were out and it was very dark.

"Thank you for your help," Tamworth said.

"That's all right, dear old Tamworth," Thomas murmured.

He had to be helped over the garden wall, and he tottered up the path holding Hedgecock and Mr. Rab. Luckily the kitchen door was still unbolted and at last he tumbled into bed.

He got up the next morning very late.

"I wonder why you're so sleepy," Mummy said. "But there was a lot of noise in the night. Animals, I think. Perhaps it kept you awake?"

"Yes, it did," Thomas agreed.

Chapter Nine

---*---

Blossom wrote out an invitation to the Minister to visit Tamworth Pig in his role of President of the Animals' Union. His campaign for growing more food was becoming more and more widely known now, and he had received a deputation from the Vegetarian League, who were most interested in his idea of eating less meat. A very handsome photograph of Tamworth seated under the damson tree appeared in the *Vegetarian Times* and Blossom cut it out and pinned it up in the Pig House, which Tamworth refused to have called a sty. "My home is not a spot on someone's eye," he declared.

In due course, the Minister's secretary wrote back to say that the Minister was very busy at present, but that he hoped to visit Baggs's Farm during the next month, and with this Tamworth had to be satisfied. He passed his time improving and decorating Pig House, and in interviewing animals who had any complaints or problems. Mr. and Mrs. Baggs remained quiet, apparently unaware of the activity going on in their orchard.

The weather continued wet and unpleasant, an English summer at its worst, but Blossom did not mind this too much because she had another interest. The Vicar's wife, new to the district and full of enthusiasm, was organizing a play to be held in the Church Hall. Blossom was to be a bear and she went around reciting her lines non-stop.

The Vicar's wife visited Mummy to see if she could help with the costumes, which she agreed to do. When the visiting lady was about to leave, having partaken of tea, six sandwiches and four cakes, she said:

"Oh, by the way, I believe you have another child as well as Blossom. Doesn't he go to school or Sunday school?"

"Well, he was ill rather a lot, so he's not going to school again till September."

"Doesn't he go to Sunday school?"

Thomas's mother didn't feel like explaining that he behaved so badly that the previous Vicar's wife had asked her not to send him any more.

"No," was all she said.

"I saw him the other day and I thought what a nice boy he looked and what a beautiful angel he'd make in the play."

"Oh, no," Mummy's voice trembled. "I don't think he'd make a good angel."

"I'm sure he'll be all right. It will be good for him. He's probably shy, and acting and singing will bring him out. Children love dressing up."

"He's a very awkward boy."

The Vicar's wife laughed.

"Nonsense, he'll be as good as gold, I'm sure. Just send him with Blossom to the rehearsal on Wednesday.

Oh, and tell him" (she wagged a forefinger) "there's a wee prize for every child taking part."

Strangely enough Thomas was quite keen, but Blossom was furious.

"I'm fed up. Oh, Mum, why did you say he could be in it? He'll spoil it. I know he'll spoil it. He always does."

"Well, perhaps he'll be good this time, dear. After all he's older now. Let's give him a chance. Be fair."

"It isn't a case of being fair. He always spoils things like this. He won't fit in with the others. He's all right with animals, but he's terrible with people. I don't know why you agreed."

"Well, honestly, I never thought he'd want to be an angel."

"It's the prize. They say it's going to be a box of chocolates and he wants one."

"Let's see how he is at the first rehearsal, anyway, Blossom. Then we can decide."

"Humph," Blossom snorted.

They returned home from the rehearsal quite late, hand in hand, eyes shining.

"Mummy, Daddy, Thomas was really good."

"I am pleased," Mummy said.

"He's chief angel."

"This I shall have to see," Daddy said.

"I was very good," the chief angel announced. "And I want four slices of toast."

"Please," Mummy and Daddy said together, automatically.

"Please," the chief angel acknowledged graciously.

Days passed. Thomas attended rehearsals, behaving beautifully. He was fitted out with a long, white robe, two tinselly wings and a halo, and spent a long time in front of mirrors, admiring himself. Blossom had a furry coat with ears and paws. She grew very nervous as the great day approached.

"I do hope I get everything right. I'm so scared," she repeated over and over again.

"I am a very good angel and I shall eat my box of chocolates all to myself," Thomas stated.

"Greedy pig," Blossom shouted.

"Don't insult me and Tamworth," Thomas roared.

He smote her several times and she fled howling.

The evening of the play arrived at last, and the children left early to be dressed and made up. By the time their parents came in, the church hall was filling rapidly, the orchestra, consisting of six recorders, two violins and a piano, was warming up unsteadily and the choir were filing into their seats.

The Vicar's wife could be seen rushing hither and thither. This was her first effort and she very much wanted it to be a success. A feeling of excitement grew with the shrilling of the recorders. The curtain went up at last to reveal a glade where a number of little bears were running about. Mummy's loving eye soon picked out Blossom, a rather plumper bear than the others. She said her lines clearly and correctly. Mummy beamed and Daddy mumbled behind his hand:

"I told you she'd be all right."

They sat back and waited for Thomas to come on.

He was one of several angels due to appear with St. Francis when he was blessing the animals. St. Francis, a portly, majestic figure in his brown sack, stood with hand outstretched over the little bears. Hand outstretched he waited . . . and waited. . . . Now was time for the angels, led by their chief, to enter from the wings and dance round the newly blessed animals, while the school orchestra burst into heavenly music and the school choir into divine song. The pianist struck the opening chords, then, like St. Francis he waited and waited . . . and struck the chord again, and waited.

From behind the scenery could be heard the ever-increasing noise of an argument. Mummy clutched Daddy's arm and one of the bears on the stage began to shuffle nervously. There was a scuffling sound and straight through the middle of the back curtains shot a strange figure. A white robe hitched around its neck half covered a red jersey, a tinsel halo hung from one ear and it seemed to be trying to pull off the wings attached to its back.

"I want my box of chocolates," the apparition shouted in a very loud voice. "I don't want a silly old book. I want a box of chocolates."

"Oh no," Daddy groaned as he battled to get to his feet, hampered by gloves, programmes, umbrellas and being in the middle of a row.

An arm, that of the Vicar's wife, came through the curtains and tried to pull back the figure.

"Come along now, do. Don't make such a scene. You're spoiling the play."

Thomas turned a look of sheer, righteous fury on her.

"You've spoilt it, you mean. You said we was goin' to get a box of chocolates and all I've got is a mouldy old book of fairy stories. It's your fault."

The audience was getting restive. Daddy had managed to reach the end of the row. Shouts of: "Get on with the play!", "Send him off!", "Shut up!", "Scotland for ever!", "Send for Tamworth Pig," boos and cheers went up.

One of the small bears ran down the stage steps sobbing dreadfully.

"I knew he would spoil it. I told and told everybody. Now will you believe me?"

Thomas stood in the centre of the stage still shouting. "Give me my box of chocolates, then I'll be an angel."

Two bears started to fight. The Vicar's wife, now struggling with Thomas, seemed to be in tears.

Daddy arrived on the stage at last, picked up the reluctant angel, still speaking loudly about his chocolates, and carried him under one arm down the gangway to the back of the hall and outside.

Above the din could be heard Lurcher Dench yelling: "Hooray for Measle Bug."

Mummy collected the weeping Blossom.

"Do you have to let us down all the time?" Daddy asked as they drove home.

"But," Thomas said, "she said she was going to give us . . ."

"We know," joined in the others, "a box of chocolates."

Thomas's voice rose above all opposition.

"She's a silly, stupid lady, that one. And that's the last time I'll be an angel."

"How right you are," Daddy replied.

Up in bed Thomas greeted Mr. Rab, Hedgecock and Num lovingly. They had been neglected of late.

"You're all right but people are stupid."

"Did you get the chocolates?" Hedgecock asked.

"Course not. Grown-ups! Huh! They always let you down. Sing the good-night song, Mr. Rab. I shall never act again."

Chapter Ten

On Baggs's Farm all was excitement. The Minister was coming! Reporters and animals were crowding into the farm. The Baggses themselves had been informed by the Minister's Secretary the previous morning and Farmer Baggs had spent the day in feverish activity, ordering gaps to be filled, gates to be repaired and extra food and vitamins for all the animals so that they would look their very best. Mrs. Baggs cleaned the house from top to bottom, dressed her dairy maids in new nylon overalls and bought herself a dress with purple flowers on it. Tamworth had an extra bucketful of food in his trough, about which he was both amused and grateful.

"I wish the Minister came every day," he said.

He'd been checking Pig House to see that it looked especially neat and tidy, and Blossom brushed him all over, which he loved. Then Thomas scratched his back for half an hour.

"I do love to be clean and well turned out," he remarked, looking at himself in Pig House mirror. "I wish people would realize this. It's not that I'm as fussy as a cat. Indeed, I'd hate to be as pernickety as some

77

cats. But I'm cleaner than a dog, for instance. I don't get fleas."

"You haven't got much to get fleas in," Thomas pointed out, looking at the spaces between the bristles.

"Don't be impertinent, Thomas."

Tamworth flipped his ears, for he was just a bit nervous and irritable.

"It's like before my birthday," Blossom said. "I just can't wait."

"But you'll just have to," Thomas replied.

"Tell us a story, Tamworth, to pass the time."

So Tamworth told them about the Greeks whom Circe the enchantress had changed into pigs, and how Odysseus, their wily leader, landed on her isle but was saved by the god Mercury, who gave him a plant to withstand her spells.

Then he told them about St. Anthony, who had a pig that he led about with a bell round its neck.

"There's a stained-glass window somewhere, showing this handsome pig," Tamworth said. "One day when St. Anthony was in Spain, he was asked to heal the King's son, but when he heard that a sow in the town had a lame and blind piglet, he healed it first before going to cure the Prince."

"He knew what was important," Thomas said.

Crowds were gathering round the farm. Photographers and reporters were wandering hither and thither. People from the Vegetarian Society had arrived by now and were walking up and down holding banners. Barry McKenzie and Joe took up their positions outside Pig House and Ethelberta was perched on the roof. Jasper and Rover were at the farmhouse, standing as quietly as Mr. and Mrs. Baggs were running up and down. Christopher Robin, arrayed in his best suit and a hideous pair of pink socks, sat moodily on the doorstep. He found it all a great bore, except that he, like Blossom, had a day's holiday from school. Gwendolyn had scarlatina, which was a good thing for everyone, except, possibly, Gwendolyn. Mummy was there with the Vicar's wife, but Daddy had refused to come, for crowds weren't in his line at all.

"Give my regards to Tamworth," he said.

Hedgecock and Mr. Rab, full of excitement, kept scuttling in and out of Pig House, and getting in Joe's way. He was so very large and always afraid of putting his huge hoofs down on something or someone small.

The warm afternoon and its crowd waited.

"It's five to three. He'll be here in a minute," Blossom said.

"Five minutes," Hedgecock corrected, accurate as ever.

A procession of cars appeared. He was early. The photographers pressed forward. A few voices called "Hurray", and the school orchestra struck up a raggedy note on six recorders, a flute and the drum, as the Minister alighted from his Rolls-Royce Silver Cloud.

He shook the hands of Mr. and Mrs. Baggs, patted Christopher's head and asked them to lead him on a tour of the farm, so off they went with a trail of people following, ruining Mrs. Baggs's herbaceous borders.

"What a wonderful place," he exclaimed, eyes dart-

79

ing everywhere over barns, animals, haystacks, milking equipment and machinery. "Beautifully kept. You are a credit to our country, Farmer er . . . er . . . er . . ."

"Baggs," his secretary whispered from behind, as he busily scribbled down notes in a little black book.

"Farmer Baggs," the Minister continued smoothly. "These fields, the hay, the wheat. . . ." Here he climbed on a gate to look down over the pleasant countryside. "It's wonderful to see the results of such industry and efficiency."

Mr. Baggs smiled broadly. He was a kind man and a good farmer. It was his wife whom nobody could bear. She stood screwing up her grey hair with her fingers.

"And now may I meet our famous Tamworth Pig, whose invitation brought me here?"

Mr. Baggs beamed. "Of course," he said as he led the way. "We're right proud of him, you know. He gets some funny ideas, he do, but there's no pig like Tamworth."

Mrs. Baggs glared out of her small, blue, beady eyes.

Tamworth was waiting, his huge beautiful shape standing firmly on his four neat little trotters. On one side was Joe, on the other Barry McKenzie with Blossom and Thomas, holding Hedgecock with Mr. Rab at his feet. Pig House was resplendent in posters, photographs of Tamworth, drawings by Blossom and pictures of food, all kinds of food except meat.

"Ah, Tamworth Pig, I presume," the Minister said, proffering his hand.

"I am deeply honoured, brother," Tamworth said

lifting a trotter. "With your permission, I should like
to speak to you alone."

The Minister frowned slightly.

"It's somewhat unusual," he said. "But then, this is
rather a special case. Let us go into your—er—sty."

"Not my sty," Tamworth's voice was gentle.
"Welcome to Pig House, brother."

They retired together and closed the door, leaving a
restless and inquiring crowd outside.

"Let's count the seconds," Hedgecock said to Thomas.

They counted up to a hundred eighteen times before the Minister and Tamworth emerged. The crowd rushed forward; Blossom and Thomas crept under Joe for shelter.

"What did you talk about? How did it go? Did you decide anything? What did you say? Have you come to an agreement?"

"We'll let you know later," the Minister smiled. "There will be a report. Right now there are tea and refreshments for everyone, being served at the farm."

There was a mad rush to the dairy where tea, biscuits, ice-cream and lemonade were being handed out by various assorted ladies and the dairy maids in their pink nylon overalls. Mrs. Baggs was charging high prices and hoping to make a good profit.

"What a lovely day," everyone said.

The lovely day was followed by one of those perfect evenings, blue and golden, that we get from time to time in England, just to remind us that it is a green and pleasant land. The Minister returned to London. The crowds went home and so did Blossom and Thomas. They played for a while and then decided to go back to Tamworth.

He was glad to see them.

"I feel restless. I can't settle down after all the excitement. I keep composing speeches and then I can't finish them. And Mrs. Baggs had a very nasty look in her eye when she brought in my food just now."

Blossom gave him some apples.

"Many thanks. I do like apples so much. But best of all, I think, I like a cabbage."

"We'll remember next time," Blossom promised.

"If you don't mind," Tamworth said, "I'd like to go for a walk. Will you come with me?"

"Yes, if I can ride on your back."

"Of course, my young friend. Leap on."

Leaping was hardly the word to describe getting on to Tamworth's back, but Thomas managed it quite well. He'd had plenty of practice.

They jogged over the fields and into the lane, Tamworth chuffing cheerily as they went along and Thomas waving hedge-parsley over them to keep off the flies.

At last Blossom said. "Just what did you and the Minister talk about, Tamworth?"

There was a roar of a powerful engine. Round the corner zoomed a motor-bike. Unable to stop, its rider crashed straight into Tamworth's huge and shapely form. The pig stood unshaken though he let out one terrible squeal. Thomas flew straight off into the ditch, full after the heavy rains, and landed squelching amid hedge-parsley, ground-ivy, foxgloves and willow-herb, to be joined by the motor-cyclist, and the pair sat glaring at each other in the ditch with garlands of up-rooted flowers round their heads while the motor-bike, far more damaged than Tamworth, lay uselessly on the grassy verge.

"Are you hurt, Tamworth?" Blossom cried. "Are you all right, Thomas?"

She ran from one to the other, waving her hands.

"I find myself undamaged," Tamworth said, after he had investigated all his trotters to see if they were still intact. "But I shall never forgive myself for that terrible squeal. It will ring in my ears till my dying day. I have never squealed in my life up till now, and I pray that I never shall again. But let us help Thomas and this unwary speedway rider out of the ditch."

However, they were already climbing out, unhurt but rather dazed, plucking flowers from their shirts, their trousers, and their shoes. The cyclist regarded the others all with horror.

"To hit a pig," he moaned. "All these years accident free and I have to hit a pig. With a boy riding it. I must be going crazy! I'm off for the police."

With difficulty he hauled up his bike and tried to start it, but no mere motor-bike could survive a head-on collision with Tamworth, so he put it down again, shook his fist at Tamworth and set off down the road.

"My good friend," Tamworth shouted, hurrying after him, "wait and see if we can help you."

It was no use, for they couldn't catch him.

"This will bring trouble," Thomas muttered, pulling a piece of willow-herb out of his mouth. "I know it will."

He was right. The motor-cyclist complained to the Sergeant at the Station, who immediately recognized Tamworth from the description. A claim was made to Farmer Baggs for the sum of one hundred pound's-worth of damage to the motor-bike caused by a menace to the public, namely a large pig with a small boy on its back.

"Pride had to come before a fall," Tamworth said. "I was too cocky after the Minister's visit."

The motor-cyclist did not get his hundred-pound claim awarded to him, but Mrs. Baggs said many nasty words and chalked up another bad mark against Tamworth.

Chapter Eleven

∗

During the following week, Tamworth was asked to appear on television. On the morning that he was due to go on, Thomas found him greatly agitated.

"What's the matter?" he asked the pig, who was scratching furiously with his front trotter.

"I've got dandruff. Horrible, itchy dandruff, I'm covered in it. There I am, about to appear before an audience of millions, and I've got dandruff. Thomas, what shall I do?"

"That's easy enough. Mother uses a medicated shampoo on us. I'll go and get it."

He shot back home and returned with a bottle of shampoo and a scrubbing brush.

"Hang on," and he once more went home to return weighed down with two buckets of water. Before Tamworth could protest he poured a bucketful straight over him.

"Ouch, ow, ow," spluttered and spat the pig, for the sudden cascade was absolutely icy. Thomas had forgotten to use the hot tap. Unmoved, he then up-ended the entire bottle of shampoo and started to scrub. He rubbed and dubbed till lather bubbled and blew in all directions. Tamworth moaned piteously. No one

would have taken him for the President at that
moment.

"It's going in my eyes."

"Mummy always tells us to be brave."

"It's difficult under such circumstances."

"Shan't be long. I've done you really well. Next
your ears. They're important. Now for the rinsing."

Thomas flung the other bucket of cold water over
the unhappy animal.

"Oh save me, someone. Help!"

No one heeded his cries and Thomas rubbed him
remorselessly with one of the best bath towels.
Mummy was rather annoyed about that when she
found out later.

"Now sit in the sun and dry. You'll feel very nice soon. I got rid of nearly all the dandruff."

Thomas inspected the shivering pig. Even his ears hung down for once, but slowly the sun warmed him and his bristles dried. He shook himself. Yes, he did feel better.

"Oh, you look beautiful. You're the handsomest as well as the cleverest pig in the world."

"You really think so?"

Tamworth loved admiration. He did, indeed, look well. His red-gold coat shone in the sun, and his ears pricked up into furry points.

"What time is the programme?"

"Eight o'clock. I've got a good showing time. The van will soon be coming to fetch me. This is a great day. I, the President of the Animals' Union, shall address the Nation."

"We'll be watching," Thomas promised.

88

Throughout the land the sets were flickering merrily before the great British public. Thomas and Blossom sat in complete harmony on the same chair, together with Hedgecock and Mr. Rab. Mummy and Daddy were also watching and so were most of the neighbours. But one household, at least, was not so pleased. Mrs. Baggs was furious that no one had asked her husband to take part in the programme. She had shaken her fist at the van that came to take Tamworth to the television studio. Christopher Robin and Lurcher had booed, but Joe, Barry McKenzie and Ethelberta chorused, "Good luck, Tamworth," as he drove away.

Mr. Baggs was not sorry at all that he had not been invited. He hated speeches and furthermore he was feeling ill that evening. He just wished his wife would stop grumbling, and that his head would stop aching. But the Baggs family, too, sat in their chairs like the rest, and watched.

At eight o'clock the Minister came on to open the programme.

"I have come here tonight to introduce my good friend, Tamworth Pig, who has some interesting schemes of his own to put forward. I do not agree with all of them, but some could bring extra prosperity to this country. However, let our eloquent friend speak for himself. Here, ladies and gentlemen, is Tamworth Pig."

Cameras panned to the handsome, porcine face with its smiling snout.

"Oh, he does look nice," Blossom whispered. "I wish we had colour television."

"I shampooed him while you were at school," Thomas hissed.

"You used my best bath towel."

Mummy was still bitter about this.

"Sh! Listen. He's about to start."

"I have come here, this evening, to ask for your help, to carry out the ideas I have in mind. Wherever we turn today we are faced with the fact that half the people of the world do not get enough to eat. Now, food is one of the best things in life. A good, tasty meal gives one a warm glow inside. Well-fed humans and animals may not be happy but at least they have a chance to be. Hungry humans and animals have no chance at all. They can only think food. They can't really think about any of the important things in life because they only feel hungry, hungry, hungry, and wonder where the next meal is coming from.

"Now in this country are many fine farmers and gardeners and food manufacturers who are doing a good job. Men like my good friend Farmer Baggs, who work hard."

" 'Ear! 'Ear!" Farmer Baggs said to his wife.

"Yet much more could be done. Let every man and woman, child and animal in the country try to produce more food, grub, as another friend of mine, Thomas, calls it."

Here Thomas went bright red and hid his face in the chair.

"Let us fill every space, every unused bit of country and waste ground in our towns, with food, oomptious, scrumptious food. I have composed a little song which goes to the tune of John Brown's body.

Let us grow more grub today, more and more and more,
Wheat and fruit and vegetables, potatoes by the score,

*With bread and cakes and sweets galore, more than you
     ever saw,*
> *Grow more grub today!*
> *Grow more, grow more,*
> *Hallelujah!*

"If you would like further details of my scheme,
including how we send extra food to other lands, I
have written a leaflet, beautifully illustrated by another
friend, Blossom."

Here it was Blossom's turn to blush.

"Including my invention of a new type of super-
heated greenhouse, and a streamlined factory for pro-
ducing an entirely new kind of sweet, invented by
myself, which does NOT make teeth decay. I have
called it Pig's Delight, and I hope that children,
especially, will like it.

"Give your animals, give us, a chance to share in the
benefits of extra food. Improve our food and we'll
improve yours even more, with better eggs, milk,
everything.

"And now I come to my final point. I am sure that
meat is bad for you. I know you love your roast
dinner but"—here Tamworth's voice trembled—
"roast pork will kill you as it will surely kill me. Let
us give you cheese, butter, milk, eggs, but not meat.
And if you ask, as well you may, well, what does a pig
give if not bacon, sausages and pork? Then I ask in
reply, do you eat your dog, your cat, your budgerigar,
your pony? Make us pigs pets like them. We shall not
disappoint you. We are clean, intelligent companions.

Make us your pets, not your dinners! May you choose wisely. I shall abide by your choice."

"Hurrah for Tamworth!" Thomas shouted.

"It's all right for you, you don't like meat. I do," Blossom said.

"It won't make a happorth of difference anyway," Daddy said. "But it was a good speech, even though he'll never get very far with it. He needs to work out his ideas more fully."

"I think I could have written a better song than he did," Mr. Rab muttered jealously to himself.

In bed, Thomas hugged Num and said, "Don't sing the bedtime song yet. I want to hear the van bring Tamworth home."

"Thomas," Mr. Rab said. "You know my special worried feeling I get. . . ."

"Humph!" Hedgecock snorted. "Rubbish."

"Well, I've got it about Tamworth," went on Mr. Rab. "There's danger about somewhere."

Just then, they all heard the van drive safely past, and so they fell asleep.

Chapter Twelve

———————————— * ————————————

Blossom, Thomas, Hedgecock and Mr. Rab were playing Ludo in the shed. They had just reached the point where Thomas was shouting with rage because Blossom had thrown three sixes in a row when there came a clatter of hoofs and a loud banging on the door. Ludo forgotten, they rushed to open. There stood Barry McKenzie Goat.

"Come. Come quick. Mrs. Baggs has captured Tamworth and locked him in the concrete hut. You know, the one beside the barns. And she's sent for the slaughterers. She says she's going to . . . to . . ."

"To what?" they cried.

"Make him into bacon and she'll eat him. Every bit. Come on."

They started to run as fast as they could towards the farm.

"What does Mr. Baggs say? Surely he won't let them kill Tamworth," Blossom panted.

"He's got 'flu and he's in bed. He doesn't know anything about it."

They ran on, red and breathless, till they reached Pig House. Blossom could not bear to look at the damson tree. Suppose Tamworth never sat there again —but that was too awful to contemplate.

"How long have we got?"

"Mr. Peasepoint, the slaughterer, lives about ten miles away. He's a busy man and he may not be able to come at once," Barry McKenzie answered.

"Is anybody guarding Tamworth?" Thomas asked.

"Christopher Robin Baggs and Lurcher Dench are on the roof armed with pitchforks."

"Oh no. How awful."

Blossom shuddered and then took a deep breath.

"We must decide on the best course of action. Barry, you fetch Joe and Fanny Cow. Thomas, you see if you can creep in to see Mr. Baggs and tell him what's going on. I'll ring up the newspapers and television studios. Surely they won't let Tamworth be killed."

"I wouldn't count on that," Hedgecock grunted. "I'm going to get a clothes-line to tie up those two boys."

"Good idea. Where shall we meet again, Blossom?" Thomas asked.

"Behind the haystack, near the shed."

Blossom ran to the nearest telephone kiosk and dialled 999.

"Which service do you require, fire, police or ambulance?" a voice asked.

"All of them! Send the lot to Baggs's Farm, Rubble Lane, where a murder is about to be committed. Hurry, please, hurry."

She banged down the receiver and ran home calling "Mummy" as she entered the house, but it was empty. She seized the directory and looked up the numbers of all the newspapers she knew.

"This is going to take some time," she murmured to herself as she put on her determined look and started dialling. "I hope Mr. Peasepoint gets a puncture in his tyres."

Meanwhile Thomas had crept quietly up to the side door of the farmhouse, which he knew was seldom used. It led to the hall and stairs. Everywhere was silent. Christopher Robin was guarding Tamworth and Mrs. Baggs was probably in the kitchen. He stole slowly up the stairs. One creaked, and, outside, Rover started to bark. Thomas paused, his heart beating so loudly he was sure someone would hear it, but no one came and he reached the landing where eight identical brown doors, all shut, confronted him. He opened one cautiously and peeped into the bathroom. He had to try all the other seven before he found the room where Mr. Baggs lay on a brass-knobbed bedstead with his eyes closed and his red face streaked with perspiration. He groaned at intervals and Thomas shook his arm.

"Mr. Baggs. You've got to get up. We need you. You've got to save Tamworth. Please wake up."

But Mr. Baggs only moaned and muttered, "Mangle worzels with the taties. Mangle worzels with the taties."

Thomas shook him again.

"Mr. Baggs! Mr. Baggs! Please wake up."

Mr. Baggs shivered so much that the eiderdown fell off the bed.

"I'm the queen of the May, Mother," he sang with the sweat running off his forehead.

Thomas wiped his face with a cloth from the bedside chair and replaced the eiderdown. It was clear that Mr. Baggs was going to be no help at all. Then he heard Mrs. Baggs coming up the stairs. He shot under the bed, trying not to breathe as she stumped round

the room. He could see her fat ankles bulging over her black-laced shoes, so he shut his eyes and prayed for her to go away. When he opened them, the feet had disappeared. He tiptoed down the stairs and out of the house. Then he ran like the wind to where the little band of rescuers was waiting.

On the shed's flat roof Lurcher and Christopher Robin were enjoying themselves hugely. They had always been afraid of Tamworth before, because he could always get at them in his field, but now he was captured and they were taking their revenge. Through a small aperture, not nearly large enough to allow Tamworth to escape, they were poking pitchforks, jabbing viciously at where they thought the pig to be.

"Yah! Fatty! Fatty Pig! Old Ginger Snout! Bristly chops! Ginger Belly! We'll have you. Take that! And that!"

They thrust and pushed and jabbed.

Tamworth sat unmoving and with immense dignity in the farthest, darkest corner. He had stuck an old piece of corrugated iron as a shield in front of himself, and was reciting a long Latin poem.

"Fatty! Are you listening, Fatty? We'll have you fried for breakfast, Fatty. Thought you were a clever pig, didn't you? Well, you're just a stupid old fool pig, aren't you? You didn't think we'd catch you, did you, Fatty?"

Tamworth spoke quietly to himself. "There are other words they could use. I can think of great, large, immense, enormous, tremendous, vast, huge, Mammoth-like, Gargantuan, Herculean, well-built, portly, ample, abundant, bulky, massive, gigantic, magnificent, leviathan, giant, mighty, corpulent, stout, plump, brawny, whacking, whopping, colossus, hippopotamus, Brobdingnagian pig, to mention a few. Then one could round off with fine, big pig."

"Shut up, Fatty. Silly ole Fatty. Who didn't know Mrs. Baggs had got a net, eh? Silly old Fatty. Caught you in it nicely, didn't she, Fatty? Yah—yah—there—take—that—and—that!"

"It was not, I admit, one of my happiest moments

98

when I was caught in the net, but a philosopher such as myself remains calm in all circumstances, however unpleasant. At least I did not squeal. I could not have forgiven myself if I had squealed."

"You'll squeal soon enough when they pig-stick you," Lurcher yelled, dancing with delight on the roof.

Suddenly he found he was dancing in the air and descending rapidly to the ground, where Joe appeared from behind the shed just in time to place one hoof, quite gently, in the middle of his back. Thomas had butted him straight off the roof. At the same time Christopher Robin Baggs, too, found himself propelled off the roof by the hands of Blossom, fierce and fighting for once with all her weight behind her. The pitchforks, Blossom's main worry, flew harmlessly through the air. She and Thomas had climbed up on to the roof behind the two boys, who were so busy shouting they'd heard nothing.

Fanny Cow waited lovingly for Christopher Robin to stand upright so that she could give him a little nudge with her horns and knock him down again, where she stood over him, chewing her cud ruminatingly. He wept, but Lurcher was made of sterner stuff and he shouted loudly:

"Mrs. Baggs! Help! Come quick, Mrs. Baggs!"

"Tie them up with the clothes-line," Hedgecock commanded and they lashed the two boys together.

"I've brought some elastoplast in case Tamworth was hurt," Blossom said.

"Put it on their mouths," Mr. Rab squeaked, quite entering into the spirit of the operation.

They did as he suggested and the boys lay silent and helpless.

But Mrs. Baggs had heard the cry for help and was now running towards them. When she saw the boys, she shrieked:

"I'll have the law on you for this."

She doubled back to the house and dialled the police station.

"Send some men to Baggs's Farm, Rubble Lane, at once."

The policeman at the other end scratched his head.

"We've already sent one lot on its way out there. Ah, well, the more the merrier."

Mrs. Baggs rushed outside again, followed by two dairy maids. Barry McKenzie and Fanny moved forward, chased them into a corner and stood over them, horns lowered.

"Get Tamworth out of there, while we hold the women back," Barry called.

Blossom fumbled with the door.

"I can't open it. It's padlocked. What shall we do?"

Then there was a noble and fearful sight. Joe turned round, backed up to the door, looking over his shoulder to judge the distance and then kicked back with his mighty hooves. The door shook, came off its hinges and fell in splinters. Pieces of wood flew over Tamworth, who sat calmly behind his corrugated-iron shield reciting this line over and over again:

"To be, or not to be, that is the question."

"Ah, my good and faithful friends. I knew you would not desert me in my hour of need."

He shook bits of shattered wood off himself and emerged from his prison. Mrs. Baggs tried to wrap her apron over Barry's horns but he tossed it back over her head.

"I'll help too," squawked Ethelberta, flying up and scurrying round in circles. "I wish I'd known all about this earlier. I've always wanted to fly on to Mrs. Baggs's head. What fun. Wheeee. Cluck-cluck."

Then, suddenly, the air was filled with the hee-hawing blare of an ambulance, followed by two police cars and a fire-engine. The whole countryside re-echoed as brakes screeched and vehicles skidded to a halt wherever they could in the farmyard. Once again Mrs. Baggs's herbaceous borders were flattened. Several uniformed men jumped out and advanced upon the scene.

"Is this Baggs's Farm?" the first policeman asked.

"Yes," everyone shouted, including Mrs. Baggs, who had managed to get the apron off her head.

"What's all the trouble, then?" he said, taking out his notebook.

Everyone rushed forward and started to speak at once, except Christopher Robin and Lurcher who were tied together on the ground, but, at that moment, the loud hee-hawing of a police car again rent the air as another contingent of constables drove into the farmyard and dismounted.

"Is this Baggs's Farm?" one of them asked.

"Yes," everyone shouted.

"What's the trouble, then?" he asked, taking out his notebook, and he advanced towards the first policeman until they almost stood face to face.

Two ambulance men emerged with a stretcher, looked round for a casualty, saw the two tied-up bodies, put them on the stretcher and disappeared with them into the ambulance.

Several firemen in search of a fire had erected ladders against the side of the house and were ascending them.

Two vans now drove up, just managing to get into the farmyard. One had "Wessex Television" on the side while the other bore the legend "Daily Moan". More men jumped out and joined the ever-increasing throng.

"Where's the TV Pig?" one man shouted.

Television cameras whirred, only to be drowned by the drone of a helicopter overhead. The BBC had arrived in style, but, unfortunately, there was no room left in the farmyard for a helicopter and they had to land in a nearby field.

The police were trying to establish some kind of order. They had persuaded Barry and Fanny Cow to allow Mrs. Baggs and her dairy maids out of their corner and now a circle formed round the silent form of Tamworth.

Blossom had seized P.C. Cubbins, a friend and ally for most of her life, and was shaking his sleeve furiously.

"She's going to kill Tamworth. You've got to stop her."

"It's my farm and my pig. Get these trespassers out of 'ere. All of 'em," Mrs. Baggs shouted, digging P.C. Spriggs with her elbow.

"She can't slaughter him, can she?" Blossom imimplored, her brown eyes wide.

"I don't know, Blossom, dear," P.C. Cubbins replied. "You see, I must do my duty."

He and P.C. Spriggs glared at one another, their chests almost meeting. It was clear which side each one favoured.

"Mrs. Baggs is entitled to do what she likes with her own property, namely one pig," Spriggs said emphatically.

Thomas glared at him, for they were old enemies.

"She's a wicked, mean woman. And Tamworth doesn't belong to her, he belongs to Farmer Baggs. You've got to see him first."

"You've got a lot to say, young Thomas," P.C. Spriggs declared. "I should think a lot of people are interfering in the Baggs's own business. And I should very much like to know who brought all this crowd here."

He stared hard and long at Blossom, who went bright red and hid her face against P.C. Cubbins's sleeve.

"Let me 'ave that pig!" Mrs. Baggs shouted.

The pig in question had a strange look on his face. He seemed to have entered into a dream, to be looking out far beyond all the farmyard turmoil.

Yet one more van squeezed into the lane and out stepped a very well-dressed gentleman with a kindly, smiling face. He pushed through the throng and came up to the main group.

"I'm Mr. Peasepoint," he beamed. "You must be Mrs. Baggs. Delighted, delighted to meet you. Dear me, what a lot of people here. I'm afraid I shall have to ask them to leave before I can carry out my good work."

Tamworth stood erect, his face altered and strange. The crowd moved back, as he spoke.

"It seems I am to die. So be it. I die for a Cause, and so I shall die proudly. I shall not squeal. Dear friends, I bid you farewell, Joe and Fanny and Barry. Don't cry, Mr. Rab. Good-bye, Hedgecock. God bless you, dearest Blossom and my esteemed friend and ally Thomas. Remember the cause, boy, remember the cause."

There was a long silence. Tears rained down Blossom's cheeks, but Thomas's eyes were blazing blue, his cheeks scarlet. He leapt, a wonderful jump, right on to Tamworth's back, where he stood shaking with fury.

"No! No! No! No! No! I won't let them kill you, Tamworth. You shan't die!"

He called up to the house, hands cupped round his mouth:

"Mr. Baggs! Mr. Baggs! Oh, do wake up, you stupid man!"

At the window above, conveniently opened by the firemen, who were still looking for the blaze, appeared the bleary visage of Farmer Baggs. He saw the crowd below, and a bewildered look spread over his face.

"Whatever's goin' on 'ere?" he said.

"That horrible, mean wife of yours is going to kill Tamworth," Thomas shouted.

Mr. Baggs paused, saw Mr. Peasepoint and he seemed to understand. The watchers below waited expectantly.

"Oh no 'er ain't. 'Er's been a-bullying of me and Tamworth for years, but 'er ain't a killing of nobody, neither me nor 'im. And now will you all go and git off my land. There ain't no peace anywhere and I want to git back to bed for me 'ead's fair a-killing of me. Maud, woman, come up yere and git me a nice, cool drop of cider. That's what 'e should be a-doing, instead of filling me farm up with foolish people with nuthin' better to do."

The window slammed shut.

Thomas collapsed on Tamworth's back and wound his arms round the stout neck. The crowd made a path for them as they turned towards Pig House with Blossom and the others following behind.

An ancient man rode up on a matching bicycle. He was the reporter from the local paper, and even as he rode in the crowd was dispersing.

"Am I late again?" he asked.

"Yes," an irritable fireman replied as he coiled up his unused hose.

"I never do get to a happening, when it's happening," the old man sighed as he remounted his machine and pedalled slowly away.

Chapter Thirteen

———————————— * ————————————

It was the last day of the summer holidays and the children had taken along sandwiches, crisps, peanuts, lemonade and chocolate to have a picnic with Tamworth. They'd prepared a special bag for him containing an assortment of apples, cabbages, carrots and turnips. Blossom danced along, eyes a-sparkle, but Thomas trailed behind moodily, kicking stones as he went.

"Cheer up. It's a lovely day and we're having a picnic with Tamworth," Blossom said.

"Don't care. Shan't cheer up. Ugh! Cheer up she says. As if anyone could cheer up with school to-morrow."

Tamworth came trotting out of Pig House to greet them.

"Hello, my friends. Why, what's the matter, Thomas?"

"I'm fed up. It's horrible old school. I don't want to go to school. I just want everything to go on like it is now, for ever and ever."

Tamworth rooted in the bag and selected the best cabbage. When he had finished it he sat down under the damson tree and looked at Thomas, who was eating nothing. Blossom had already eaten four sandwiches and a bag of crisps.

"Oh, Thomas," he said. "Everything changes. It has to. It's the way of things. It won't be so bad at school, in fact, you'll enjoy it once you're there again."

"The only things I shall enjoy are bashing old Baggsy and pulling Gwendolyn horrible Twitchie's hair."

"You mean horrible hair," Hedgecock put in.

"No I don't. I mean Gwendolyn, horrible, Twitchie," Thomas snapped.

"Well, I know something you'll like," Tamworth said.

He went into Pig House and emerged with a football, dribbling it mostly between his trotters.

"Where did you get that?" Blossom asked, her mouth full of chocolate.

She'd almost finished her share of the picnic.

"It was sent to me by one of my many admirers. Come on, everyone. We're going to play football and give Thomas lots of practice."

Thomas still looked sulky, so Tamworth flipped the ball at him with his snout. He looked so funny that a grin began to spread over Thomas's face, and he too, ran forward, took a mighty kick and sent the ball high over Pig House. In no time at all, two sweaters were down as goal posts and everyone was running and kicking like mad.

At last Tamworth stopped, puffing like a steam-engine.

"I'm losing pounds of beautiful fat. I shall have to

have some more sustenance," he panted, as he searched
in the bag for another cabbage.

Everyone collapsed, red, sweaty and cheerful, and
finished the rest of the picnic.

"And now I've got another surprise for you. Come
into Pig House," Tamworth said.

They went inside, and there on a box stood a tran-
sistor radio. Tamworth turned the knob and music
blared forth.

"It's a beauty. Where did you get it?" Mr. Rab
asked.

"The Vegetarian Society presented it to me for my
work in trying to stop people eating meat."

He looked very pleased with himself.

"I want you to listen to the news, which is on in a minute. Sit down all of you."

They sat down and listened quietly. At last the music stopped and the newsreader came on. He read out several items of news and Mr. Rab began to fidget because he found it boring, but Hedgecock nudged him sharply. Then came the item Tamworth was waiting for and he turned up the volume.

"After a debate in Parliament yesterday, it was decided to start a campaign for 'Grow more food' in Britain. A committee has been set up to promote food expansion and it will be advised by Tamworth Pig of Baggs's Farm."

"There," Tamworth said, and switched off the radio.

"Why, Tamworth, you've gone pink under your bristles!" Blossom said.

"Yes, I'm very pleased that my small efforts have not gone unnoticed. And I owe so much of this to you, dear friends."

He took the lid off a cardboard box and emptied out several parcels, all wrapped in blue and red paper decorated with white dancing pigs.

"So I have presents for you all. The Vicar's wife was kind enough to purchase them for me."

Blossom opened hers first and there inside was the prettiest, floppiest doll ever, with hair so soft you wanted to rub your face in it. She wore a little white gown with a blue ribbon round it to match her eyes.

"Oh, oh," was all Blossom could say.

She felt as if she could cry, it was so beautiful.

For Thomas there was a gloriously complicated train set with lots of points, gradients, stations, signals, engines and rolling stock. Mr. Rab had a book containing hundreds and hundreds of poems and for Hedgecock there was a compendium of games, including chess, draughts, ludo, snakes and ladders, tiddlywinks and dominoes.

They could hardly speak, it was such a surprise. Tamworth trotted back and forth poking his snout into everything, enjoying the presents just as much as they did, and he simultaneously played games with Hedgecock, dolls with Blossom, trains with Thomas and listened to Mr. Rab reading from his book.

Then he routed around in the box and pulled out one last parcel.

"The Vicar's wife also sent something else for you, Thomas. She says she hopes you'll be friends again."

With a huge grin, he handed over a box of chocolates.